OCTONAUTS

D1296304

and the Whitetip Shark

OCTONAUTS WHO'S WHO

The daring crew of the Octopod are ready to embark on an exciting new mission!

INKLING OCTOPUS
(Professor)

KWAZII CAT
(Lieutenant)

PESO PENGUIN
(Medic)

BARNACLES BEAR
(Captain)

TWEAK BUNNY
(Engineer)

SHELLINGTON SEA OTTER
(Field Researcher)

DASHI DOG
(Photographer)

TUNIP THE VEGIMAL
(Ship's Cook)

EXPLORE . RESCUE . PROTECT

OCTONAUTS™

and the Whitetip Shark

SIMON AND SCHUSTER

Captain Barnacles had an exciting
new mission for the Octonauts.
"We need to find out what kind of
sharks visit this reef," he announced.
Shellington grinned. He couldn't
wait to study a shark up close!
"Not too close," gulped Peso.
"Sharks can be dangerous."

Kwazii grinned, "And that's why I can't wait to get going and…"

"Clean the gups?" Captain Barnacles asked. "Our gups are covered in gunk and they don't work well when they're dirty."

"Aye, aye," groaned Kwazii. "But I'd rather be swimming with the sharks!"

Barnacles, Peso and Shellington climbed aboard the Gup-A.

The GUP-A chugged through the ocean.
A stripy fish peeped out of the shadows.

"Look! There's a pilot fish," said
Shellington. "No sharks though."

"Let's move further down the reef,"
decided Captain Barnacles.

No one noticed the
pilot fish dart up
and nibble at the
bottom of
the GUP-A.

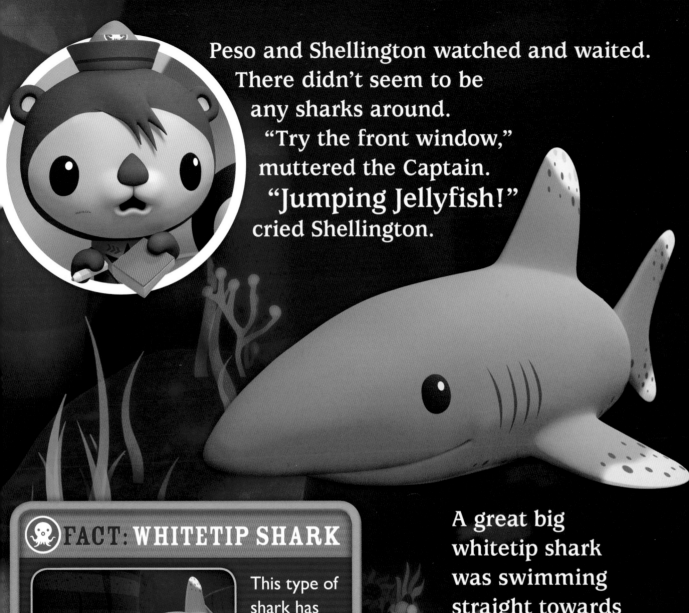

Peso and Shellington watched and waited. There didn't seem to be any sharks around. "Try the front window," muttered the Captain. "Jumping Jellyfish!" cried Shellington.

A great big whitetip shark was swimming straight towards the GUP-A!

FACT: WHITETIP SHARK

This type of shark has white tips on its fins.

The whitetip shark opened its massive mouth.
  "Look at those teeth," remarked Shellington.
  "It could use a toothbrush!"
  Suddenly the shark grabbed the GUP-A's light
and thrashed its tail.

"What's he trying to do?" gasped Peso.
  Shellington frowned. "He's trying to take a bite
out of the gup!"

"The shark could hurt himself and us," cried Captain Barnacles. "Hold on!" Barnacles tried to get the Gup-A free of the shark.

The whitetip shark chased the Octonauts. The little pilot fish followed too.

Put-put-put!

The Gup-A spluttered to a stop.

"Some gunk must have got in the propeller," said the Captain.

Finally he got the sub started again and they pulled away just in time!

Back on the Octopod, Professor Inkling and Kwazii were playing table tennis.

"This is easier for you!" cried Kwazii, hitting the ball.

The Professor laughed. Even with eight tentacles and four bats, Kwazii was impossible to beat.

Time was ticking away, and Kwazii was supposed to be cleaning the gups, but he was having too much fun.

"Just one more game," he said, "against all of you!"
Professor Inkling,
Tweak and Tunip
grabbed their paddles.

"You're on!"

The table tennis match was getting exciting.

"The next point wins," Kwazii grinned.

He glanced out of the window. Was that the Gup-A having a grand adventure chasing after a whitetip shark?

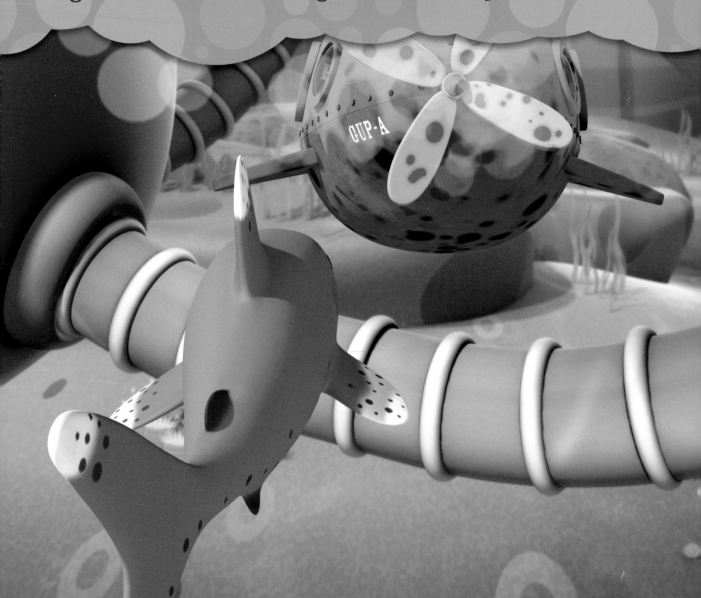

The Octonauts
peered through the glass.
  "They're not chasing that shark,"
shouted Dashi. "That shark is chasing them!"
  Not only was the shark chasing the GUP-A, it was starting
to catch up!
  "We can't shake him," said the Captain. "Peso, sound
the Octoalert!"

"Octonauts, to

your stations!"

Tweak opened the Octohatch. As soon as the GUP-A was in she closed the door again, shutting the shark outside! The crew were relieved to be back in the launch bay.

"That will teach me to take out a gunky gup," sighed the Captain.

"How's the cleaning coming along, Kwazii?"

"I haven't started... I mean **finished** yet, Captain" admitted the sea cat.

Kwazii hurried back to work.

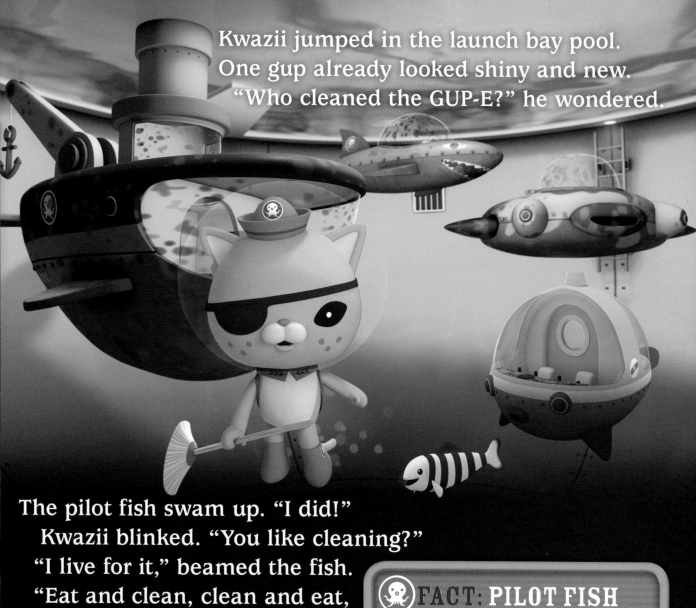

Kwazii jumped in the launch bay pool.
One gup already looked shiny and new.
"Who cleaned the GUP-E?" he wondered.

The pilot fish swam up. "I did!"
  Kwazii blinked. "You like cleaning?"
  "I live for it," beamed the fish.
  "Eat and clean, clean and eat,
you know how it is!"
  "Ha ha!" laughed Kwazii.
"Dinner is served!"

FACT: **PILOT FISH**

Pilot fish get their food by eating gunk off of things.

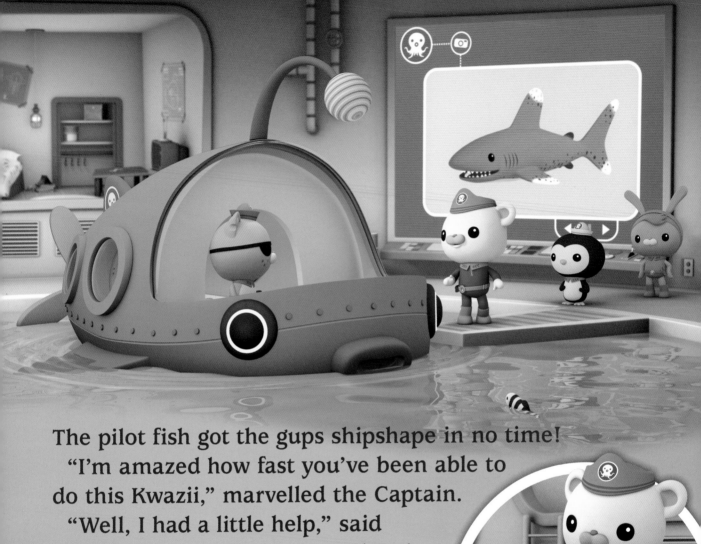

The pilot fish got the gups shipshape in no time!

"I'm amazed how fast you've been able to do this Kwazii," marvelled the Captain.

"Well, I had a little help," said Kwazii, introducing his new cleaning assistant.

"I'm still hungry," said the pilot fish. "Usually I clean sharks."

Barnacles remembered the shark on the reef. His teeth were very dirty.

The Octonauts decided to help the pilot fish find the whitetip shark.

"Open the Octohatch!" cried Barnacles.

Kwazii wasn't missing this mission. It definitely beat cleaning gups!

The pilot fish led the GUP-A back out to the reef.

"Oh!" gasped Peso. **"Sh-sh-shark!"**

The shark looked angry. It bit on the GUP-A's light then snapped at the portholes.

"Time to eat and clean," said the pilot fish. "Open wide, buddy!"

"Maybe this wasn't such a good idea," squeaked Peso. But instead of eating the pilot fish, the shark let him clean his teeth!

🐙 FACT: PROTECTION

Sharks offer pilot fish protection in return for cleaning their teeth.

"That's better," the whitetip shark grinned.
"You're just the little fellow I need."
"Thanks Octonauts!" shouted the pilot fish, swimming away with his new friend.

"I'm going to miss him," sighed Kwazii. "I'll have to clean the gups by myself next time."
The friends chuckled all the way back to the Octopod.

☤ CAPTAIN'S LOG:

Calling all Octonauts! Our mission to the reef was our most dangerous yet, but we learned something unusual. Who would have thought that a tiny pilot fish would make friends with a fierce, whitetip shark?

FACT FILE: **THE WHITETIP SHARK AND PILOT FISH**

The pilot fish and whitetip shark have a special friendship. The pilot fish follows the shark wherever it goes, eating and cleaning the gunk from its teeth.

They live in open water.

The whitetip shark eats fish and squid.

The pilot fish eats the shark's leftovers.

OCTOFACTS:

1. Pilot fish and sharks help each other.

2. The pilot fish keeps the shark's teeth clean and the shark scares away other fish that might try to eat the pilot fish.

3. Sometimes a whole shoal of pilot fish will live and swim with one shark.

OCTONAUTS™

Calling all Octonauts! Get ready to discover an ocean full of thrilling new books...

and the Decorator Crab

and the Whale Shark

The Amazing Octopod
A Pop-Up and Play Adventure

and the Giant Squid

and the Electric Torpedo Rays

and the Flying Fish

and the Orcas

and the Whitetip Shark

and the Scary Spookfish

and the Undersea Eruption

and the Great Christmas Rescue!

and the Marine Iguanas
A Lift-the-Flap Adventure!

Octopod Adventure
Drive the Octopod through the ocean deep!

and the Monster Map
A Lift-the-Flap Adventure!

and the Great Penguin Race

Meet the Crew

Go Go Gups!

Ready for Action in the GUP – A!

Ready to Race in the GUP – B!

Little Library

to the Rescue!
Sticker Scene Book

www.theOctonauts.com
www.simonandschuster.co.uk